This book is lovingly dedicated to our children,

with boundless appreciation for their

continuous encouragement and support.

ISBN: 0-97225703-9
13-Digit: 978-0-97225703-9

Published by:

www.deertales.com

Typesetting by Julie Melton, The Right Type Graphics (USA)

Printed in China

2008

The White Fawn

By Karen Collett Wilson

Photography by Susan A. Zerga

Karen Collett Wilson

Susan Zerga

Did I ever tell you the story of the amazing fawn that appeared in our Cottonwoods not long ago? Gather near, and I'll tell you what happened.

It all began in the spring of the year. That is the season when the snow banks have melted and the birds have returned from their winter migration.

It is the season of wild flowers.

It is also the time when the animal babies are born in the Cottonwoods. Fawns are born with a brown coat of hair that has white spots along the back and sides. This coloring blends with the grasses and low bushes in the Cottonwoods. It is this camouflage that protects them.

That spring, a fawn was born with unusual coloring. His peculiar white coat was very curious. He looked so different from the other fawns that the animals of the Cottonwoods did not know what to think of him.

The lumbering cow mothers told their calves that he was the color of frosty snow, and therefore, he must be cold and unfriendly.

The jittery raccoon mother told her nursery of kits that he was the color of clouds before a noisy thunderstorm, and he must be boisterous as well.

The broody mare told her foal that he was the color of ash after a range fire, and he must be dangerous.

The turkey hen told her poults that he was the color of the streaking hawk as it swoops after prey, and he must not be trusted.

The sensible owl told her owlet that he was the color of dust blown by a brisk spring wind, and he must be flighty and silly.

The wooly ewe told her lambs that he was the color of ripples on the rushing creek, and he must be rowdy.

The wandering cat thought he was a ghostly wood-sprite and simply something to hiss at.

The skunks decided they were in no position to criticize, and they didn't say a word.

But the babies of the Cottonwoods decided they would find out for themselves about the extraordinary fawn.

They played with him and spent time getting to know him.
They soon discovered he was friendly and fun.

They learned that he was not dangerous or silly, and he could be trusted.

The animal mothers soon discovered he was just as playful and pesky, just as sweet and lovable as all of their babies.

To this day, no one knows why the fawn arrived with a surprising coat… and what's more, they don't even care!

Other books by

Karen Collett Wilson

and

Susan A. Zerga

Pogonip Magic

Autumn Rescue

The Curious Adventure: A Summer Deer Tale